Mermaid Alert

Jessica stopped to catch her breath. "I saw something amazing!"

"Another giant squid?" Winston asked, laughing.

"No, this is for real," Jessica said. "I saw a real live mermaid."

There was a stunned silence. Then a lot of kids burst out laughing. Even Mrs. Otis chuckled.

"Good joke, Jessica," the teacher said with a smile. "That's the best one yet. Now let's continue looking for different kinds of seaweed."

Everyone turned away from Jessica and went back to their seaweed search.

Jessica couldn't believe no one was taking her seriously. She opened her mouth to say something else, but nothing came out.

Bantam Books in the SWEET VALLEY KIDS series

SWEET VALLEY KIDS

JESSICA'S MERMAID

Written by
Molly Mia Stewart

Created by
FRANCINE PASCAL

Illustrated by
Ying-Hwa Hu

BANTAM BOOKS
NEW YORK • TORONTO • LONDON • SYDNEY • AUCKLAND

To William Francis Robb IV

RL 2, 005-008

JESSICA'S MERMAID
A Bantam Book / May 1994

*Sweet Valley High® and Sweet Valley Kids are
trademarks of Francine Pascal*

Conceived by Francine Pascal

*Produced by Daniel Weiss Associates, Inc.
33 West 17th Street
New York, NY 10011*

Cover art by Susan Tang

ISBN: 0-553-48118-5

Published simultaneously in the United States and Canada

Bantam Books are published by Bantam Books, a division of Bantam
Doubleday Dell Publishing Group, Inc. Its trademark, consisting of the
words "Bantam Books" and the portrayal of a rooster, is Registered in
U.S. Patent and Trademark Office and in other countries. *Marca
Registrada.* Bantam Books, 1540 Broadway, New York, New York 10036.

PRINTED IN THE UNITED STATES OF AMERICA

CWO   0 9 8 7 6 5 4 3 2 1

CHAPTER 1

A Giant Sea Monster

Elizabeth Wakefield went to the rear of her second-grade classroom and leaned down to look into the hamsters' cage. "Hi, Tinkerbell, hi, Thumbelina," she said, waving her fingers. "Did you have a nice weekend?"

The two identical hamsters sat back on their hind legs and stared at Elizabeth with puzzled looks. There was a lot of noise in Mrs. Otis's classroom. Kids were filing in, all talking excitedly. Next to Elizabeth, her twin sister, Jessica, put her face close to the cage too.

"I can never tell who's who," Jessica said.

Elizabeth giggled. "That's what people say about us."

On the outside, Elizabeth and Jessica looked exactly the same. Both girls had blue-green eyes and long blond hair with bangs. When they wore matching outfits, most of their classmates at Sweet Valley Elementary School had trouble telling them apart. But it was easy to tell who was who if you looked at the twins' name bracelets, or if you knew the twins each had their own likes and dislikes.

That's because on the *inside* Elizabeth

and Jessica were very different. Each girl had her own special personality. Elizabeth loved reading, making up adventure stories, and playing all kinds of sports. She was especially proud to be a member of the Sweet Valley Soccer League. Jessica didn't like games that got her clothes dirty. She preferred playing with dolls, and pretending to be a princess. She loved being the center of attention.

But despite their differences, Elizabeth and Jessica were best friends. They shared a bedroom, toys, chores, and secrets.

"Look at Lila," Jessica said, glancing back toward the front of the room. "She's showing off. As usual."

"My father has been to Hawaii seven

times," Lila Fowler was saying. "This time he brought me this seashell necklace." She fingered the necklace around her throat. "Isn't it beautiful?"

"It is," Ellen Riteman, a pretty girl with brown hair, said. "Maybe I could make one."

"And one for me, too," Amy Sutton said.

"No way." Lila crossed her arms in front of her chest. "You can't find these shells in California. You have to travel far." Lila's father was one of the wealthiest people in Sweet Valley, and she always let everyone know it.

"Your necklace is pretty," Eva Simpson said. "But in Jamaica you can find stranger-looking shells. I've got a lot of them at home." Eva had moved to Sweet Valley from Jamaica, an island in the Caribbean. Lila didn't impress her too much.

"Well, I've never seen you wearing a necklace of those strange shells," Lila said. "So what good are they?"

"It's a collection," Elizabeth said, joining her friends. "I've seen—" She felt someone tug on her elbow. It was Jessica.

"Look!" Jessica said, pointing out the window. "There's a horse!"

"On the playground?" Elizabeth asked in surprise.

"Where?" asked Lois Waller, running to the window. "I don't see anything." Lois was chubby and often got teased by the boys.

5

"Made you look!" Jessica said with a grin.

"Ha ha," Elizabeth said.

Lila waited for the group to gather around her again. "For my tenth birthday my dad says he'll take me to Hawaii for a real luau."

"That's not for another three years, Lila," Elizabeth said. "Maybe your dad will forget."

"Yeah," Jessica agreed. "Big deal." She looked over at the door to the hall. "There's Mrs. Armstrong!" she exclaimed. Mrs. Armstrong was Sweet Valley Elementary School's principal. "She dyed her hair green!"

"You're kidding!" Elizabeth whirled around. There was no green-haired principal in sight. She noticed Jessica's eyes twinkling.

"Very funny," Elizabeth said with a laugh. "You're just trying to get attention away from Lila," she added in a whisper.

Jessica shrugged. "Maybe I am, maybe I'm not," she said.

"Well, you can say whatever you want," Elizabeth replied. "I'm so excited about our field trip today that I don't care if Mrs. Armstrong's hair is green or purple."

Mrs. Otis's class was going to the Wild Seashore Preserve. The preserve was an hour from Sweet Valley by bus. Elizabeth had been looking forward to it for weeks. She knew there would be sea lions and otters and all kinds of birds and fish.

"Well, Mrs. Armstrong's hair isn't really green," Jessica admitted. Then she looked out the window and her eyes widened. "But that giant sea monster is!"

Elizabeth laughed again. "I hope we do see a sea monster today," she said, refusing to look out the window. "This is going to be a great field trip."

CHAPTER 2

A Giant Squid

When it was time to climb aboard the bus, Jessica made sure she was the first on line. She wanted to save seats for all her friends.

"Come back here," Jessica shouted as she raced for the rear of the bus, and bounced up and down on the last seat. "Hurry!"

Elizabeth, Lila, Ellen, Amy, and Eva did their best to rush down the aisle, but everyone was scrambling for a seat.

And everyone was laughing and talking loudly. Even Mrs. Otis was adding to the noise as she talked to the bus driver.

"Whew! That was like a human obstacle course," Elizabeth said when she finally reached Jessica. She plopped down next to her sister. Their friends took seats ahead of them and to the side.

"This is going to be so much fun!" Jessica said. She looked down at her feet and frowned. "But I wish my new shoes weren't so tight."

Elizabeth shook her head. "I told you not to wear your new clothes on a field trip. You're lucky Mom didn't see you leave the house. You'll get in trouble if you ruin them."

"I like my new clothes," Jessica said, sticking out her feet and admiring the shiny buckles on her shoes. She was wearing a new sailor outfit and a new pair of patent-leather shoes. Mrs. Wakefield had bought the same outfit and shoes for both of the twins over the weekend. Elizabeth's sailor suit was hanging neatly in her bedroom closet, though, and her shiny shoes were still in their box. But Jessica had wanted to wear her suit and shoes as soon as possible.

All the other kids were wearing shorts and T-shirts and sneakers. Jessica knew she was the best-dressed girl in the class that day. But so far, nobody had even noticed. They were too excited about the trip to the Wild Seashore Preserve.

"Did you see my new shoes?" Jessica asked Ellen.

Ellen was busy talking to Amy about seashells. "What?" she asked as she turned around.

"Did you see my new shoes?" Jessica repeated with a smile.

Ellen and Amy leaned over the back of their seat to look. "They're pretty, Jessica," Ellen said. She shrugged. "But you're crazy to wear them to the beach."

Amy giggled. "Yeah, not a great idea," she said.

Jessica sat back and looked grumpily out the window.

"Ellen thinks she can find the same shells that are on Lila's Hawaiian necklace," Amy announced.

13

"That's impossible," Lila said from across the aisle. She pointed to the middle shell on her necklace. It was a smooth yellow one. "This is a very rare kind of cowrie shell. You could never find it. It's extra special."

"I still think I can find all the shells," Ellen said. "Even the cowrie."

"I bet Ellen can," Elizabeth agreed. "She knows more about shells than anyone in our whole class."

Lila shook her head. "No way."

"Why is everyone talking about Lila's stupid necklace?" Jessica grumbled as she slumped down in the seat.

No one heard her. And no one paid attention to her. Lila continued to brag about her necklace. Ellen continued to say she could find every shell and make an identical necklace. Amy, Eva, and Elizabeth continued to encourage Ellen.

Jessica looked out the window, feeling left out. She wished her friends would pay attention to her. After all, she was wearing new clothes.

"Look!" Jessica shouted. "A giant squid!"

The conversation stopped. Everyone looked out the window, and then at Jessica.

"Fooled you," Jessica said with a smile.

"Whoop-de-do," Lila said. "You're so silly, Jessica."

Winston Egbert, the class clown, began waving his arms around. "I'm the giant squid!" he said in a deep voice from the middle of the bus. "I am going to get you!"

Everyone laughed—everyone except Jessica. She was tired of being ignored and did not appreciate having people say she was silly.

"Why do you keep saying 'look' all the time?" Elizabeth asked. "It's dumb."

"I don't know," Jessica said. "I guess *I* think it's funny."

"Well, it's not," Elizabeth said, frowning. "You're just trying to get attention."

Jessica looked away and folded her arms. She was beginning to wish she could start the whole day over.

CHAPTER 3

The Wrong Shoes

As the bus got closer to the preserve, Elizabeth was too excited about the field trip to sit still.

"I think we're almost there," she said as the bus began to slow down. "We are! There's the sign!"

In front of them was a large wooden sign that read WELCOME TO THE WILD SEASHORE PRESERVE: NO SWIMMING, SURFING, MOTORBOATS, PLANT COLLECTING, OR LITTERING. PLEASE DO NOT FEED THE ANIMALS!

Mrs. Otis stood up. "Listen up, kids!" she said as the bus pulled into a parking space. "Our guide will be taking us on a walking tour. Please remember to follow the rules. If you have questions, please ask. Now, let's get out and form a group in the parking lot. Don't forget your lunch bags!"

"Yippee!" Elizabeth said. She retied her sneakers. "I hope we see otters and pelicans and everything!"

Pushing and jostling, the kids exited the bus. The sun shone, and a salty breeze blew in from the ocean. Gulls squawked, and there was a roar of waves crashing on rocks.

As the class assembled in the parking lot, a young man in shorts and a safari jacket walked over to join them.

"Hello, my name is Travis McCabe," he said, shaking Mrs. Otis's hand. He turned to the class. "Please call me Travis. Welcome to a day of exploring the beach. Are you all ready?"

"YES!" everyone shouted.

Travis looked around and noticed Jessica. "Do you have some other shoes?" he asked. "The trail is pretty rough."

Some of the boys giggled. Jessica shook her head. "I like my shoes. They're very comfortable," she said, looking embarrassed.

Travis nodded doubtfully. "You can always take your shoes off," he said, "but I suggest that you keep them on as much as possible. That goes for everyone. You never know when there'll be a sharp shell in the sand, and you also want to keep your hands free. I'm glad most of you brought your lunch and other things in knapsacks."

Elizabeth nudged Jessica with her elbow. "I'll carry the knapsack we brought. And maybe we can trade shoes later," she said.

"Thanks for carrying our stuff," Jessica replied. "But no thanks about the shoes. I don't want to trade."

Ellen held up her hand. "Can we collect shells?" she asked. "I want to make a necklace—just like Lila's." She pointed at Lila, who glared back at her.

"Certainly," Travis said. "You can take home any empty shells you find. If a shell is empty, there's no animal living inside it anymore. Now, the area I'm taking you to is a protected environment. That means it is against the law to harm any of the animals and plants living there." He pointed behind him. "Stay on the path until we get to the beach. We have a long hike ahead of us before we get to Seal Beach, where we'll have lunch."

"Seals!" Elizabeth said, jumping up and down. "Yay!"

At last, the best part of their trip was about to begin. The kids followed Travis single-file through a gate. He led them through a rocky area with short, twisted pine trees and bright yellow flowers. The air had a spicy smell, and birds darted in and out between the rocks. As they walked, the sound of the ocean grew louder and louder.

Then the path went around a corner, and they saw the ocean below. There were rocks and waves and a sandy beach.

"The path is steep, so don't run," Travis warned.

Elizabeth looked back at Jessica, who was at the end of the line. She was dragging her feet. Elizabeth waited for her.

"Isn't this fun?" Elizabeth asked when Jessica caught up to her. "Did you see those beautiful flowers?"

"No," Jessica said. Her skirt snagged on a thorn, and she stopped to untangle it. "It's hot, and my feet hurt."

"Just try to forget about them," Elizabeth suggested. "Come on, let's catch up."

Together, they reached the beach. Ahead of them, Ellen bent down at the edge of a tidal pool.

"Look, here's one of the shells from Lila's necklace!" she exclaimed, holding up a pink scallop shell.

Elizabeth joined Ellen at the pool. There was a hollowed-out place in the rocks where water had collected.

"Oh, a yellow starfish!" Elizabeth said in amazement. "Wow, it's moving its arms!"

She looked back. Jessica was walking slowly, looking at the ground.

"Are you trying to find shells, Jess?" Elizabeth asked.

"No," Jessica grumbled.

Elizabeth sighed. "Try to cheer up.

How about coming with me to listen to Travis talk about nature facts?"

"Go without me," Jessica said. "I don't care."

Elizabeth hesitated for a moment. She could tell that her sister was sorry for wearing the wrong clothes, and for acting so silly all morning. But it was too late to change things now.

Besides, she didn't want to miss a single part of the visit to the seashore.

"OK. I'll see you later," Elizabeth said. She hurried off to join the others.

CHAPTER 4

What Jessica Sees

Jessica let out a heavy sigh as she dragged her feet to join her classmates. She wished someone would come back to walk with her. Up ahead, she heard Lila still bragging about her necklace, and Ellen teasing Lila about it. All of Jessica's friends were climbing on rocks and chasing each other through the sand.

But nobody seemed to care where Jessica was. Even Elizabeth had gone ahead without her, and all Lila and

Ellen cared about was their stupid shells, Jessica thought. She stopped and sat down on a rock.

Her feet were hot, and there was sand in her shoes.

"I'm getting a blister," Jessica said mournfully. She rested her chin in her hand. "Why did I wear these clothes?"

She sniffed back a tear, then took off her shoes and socks and poured the sand out of them. Beside her, the water in a large tidal pool looked cool and refreshing.

Jessica glanced back toward her classmates. They were starting to look like specks in the distance. No one was around. Jessica knew there was no swimming allowed, but maybe it would be all right if she just dipped her feet in the water. That was sure to cool them off.

She stuffed her socks in her shoes and held them in one hand. Then she walked carefully across the smooth rocks to the tidal pool. There was one rock where she could sit and paddle her feet. Sunlight bounced off the water into her eyes, making it hard to see.

Jessica squinted, trying to determine how deep the pool was. All of a sudden, she realized she was looking into a pair of large, brown eyes framed by long, flowing hair.

"Oh!" Jessica gasped.

There was a splash, and in an instant, the eyes and hair vanished. Jessica bent down for a closer look. Through the dazzling water, she saw the faint shadow of a long, graceful tail. Then it was gone.

In astonishment, Jessica dropped her shoes and rubbed her eyes.

"Was that a mermaid?" she whispered out loud.

Jessica stared at the tidal pool. But the sun was so bright, she couldn't see beneath the surface of the water.

"Beautiful eyes, long hair, graceful body . . . a tail . . ." Jessica listed what she had seen. She swallowed hard. It was almost too good to be true.

"I did see a mermaid!" she said excitedly.

She hastily put her socks and shoes back on. "Now they'll pay attention to me!" she told herself happily.

As soon as she had her shoes buckled,

Jessica raced along the beach after her classmates. It took her a while to catch up, but once she did, nothing could make her stop talking.

"Wait up! Wait up!" Jessica yelled.

The group halted. Mrs. Otis and Travis walked toward her with concerned looks.

"Are you hurt, Jessica?" Mrs. Otis asked. "I was starting to wonder what had happened to you." Jessica's friends gathered around.

Jessica stopped to catch her breath. "No," she panted, looking at everyone with a wide smile. "I saw something amazing!"

"Another giant squid?" Winston said, laughing.

"No, this is for real," Jessica said.

She paused, glad to see how interested everyone was.

"So what did you see?" Elizabeth asked.

"A mermaid!" Jessica announced triumphantly. "I saw a real live mermaid."

There was a stunned silence. Then a lot of the kids burst out laughing. Even Mrs. Otis chuckled.

"Good joke, Jessica," the teacher said with a smile. "That's the best one yet. Now, let's continue looking for different kinds of seaweed."

Everyone turned away from Jessica and went back to their seaweed search.

Jessica couldn't believe no one was taking her seriously. She opened her mouth to say something else, but nothing came out.

CHAPTER 5

The Girl Who Cried Mermaid

Elizabeth was the only one still standing near Jessica. She saw that her sister looked terribly disappointed. The waves rolled in on the beach, and the breeze blew across their cheeks. Elizabeth tried to find a twinkle in Jessica's eyes—a twinkle that meant she was joking. There wasn't any.

"You believe me, don't you?" Jessica asked. "You believe I really saw a mermaid?"

"No," Elizabeth said, shaking her head. "All day you've been telling everyone to look at things that aren't there. Anyway, I don't believe in mermaids."

"But I'm not making it up," Jessica said, grabbing Elizabeth's hand. "All those other times I was just kidding around, but now it's for real. Honest, truly, really."

Elizabeth nudged a broken seashell with her foot. Jessica sounded truthful. But Jessica was very good at fooling people.

"Please, Lizzie, you've got to believe me," Jessica begged. She tugged on Elizabeth's hand. "I'll show you."

"No," Elizabeth said firmly. She pulled her hand away. "As soon as I say I believe you, you'll just laugh and say you tricked me. It's not funny anymore."

"But it's not a trick!" Jessica's eyes filled with tears.

Elizabeth suddenly had a strange, un-comfortable feeling. She was sure Jessica was kidding. She knew Jessica could fake tears when she wanted to. But on the other hand, maybe Jessica *had* seen some-thing. Not a mermaid, but something.

"Everyone's being so mean to me," Jessica whined. She sat down and threw a handful of sand up into the air.

Elizabeth shook her head. "You're just crabby because you wore the wrong clothes and you can't hike around the way the rest of us can. But all your silly stories aren't going to make us pay attention to you. So stop

acting like a baby and come have fun."

"I am not acting like a baby," Jessica said, standing up. She stomped her foot in the sand. "I know what I saw. And I saw a mermaid!"

Elizabeth backed up slowly. "Remember the story about the boy who cried wolf?" she said. "He kept shouting to the other shepherds that his sheep were being attacked by a wolf. Only, it wasn't true. When his friends came running to help, he just laughed at them. He did it so many times that when a wolf really did attack his sheep, nobody came when he shouted. That's what you did, Jessica. You were crying wolf, and I'm not going to look again."

She turned her back on Jessica and ran down to her friends near the water.

CHAPTER 6

All Alone

Jessica sat down on a rock and squeezed her eyes shut. She tried to remember exactly what she had seen. There was the pair of beautiful brown eyes, the long, flowing hair, and the flick of a tail.

"I'm not making it up," Jessica said firmly. She wiped a tear from her eye and stood up. It wasn't going to be easy, she thought, but she was going to try one last time to convince the others that she had seen a mermaid.

"Ellen," she called out, running up to her friend.

Ellen was walking slowly, keeping a sharp lookout for shells. "Look," Ellen said as Jessica ran up to her. She held out her hands. "I have all the shells from Lila's necklace, except for the yellow cowrie."

"Good," Jessica said. "I hope you do find it. That'll show Lila." She had an idea. "Ellen, if I help you find the shell, will you believe me about the mermaid?"

Ellen frowned. "There's no mermaid back there," she said. "You're just making it up."

"But I'm not," Jessica insisted.

Up ahead, Travis called for a halt. "This is Seal Beach," he said. "This is where we'll have our lunch."

"I don't see any seals," Todd said.

"Maybe they're having their lunch in the ocean," Elizabeth suggested.

"That's a good guess," Travis agreed. "We might see some by the time we finish eating."

The class spread out on the beach. Some sat in the warm sand, and others climbed onto the boulders. Jessica noticed Lois sitting with Julie Porter. She walked over to them.

"Hi, Jessica," Lois said. "Do you want to eat with us?"

"Do you believe me about the mermaid?" Jessica asked.

39

Julie twirled her finger next to her ear. "No way!"

"What about you, Lois?" Jessica asked.

"Well . . ." Lois took her sandwich out of her knapsack. "You said there was a horse in the playground this morning, and that wasn't true. So I guess I don't believe you."

Frowning, Jessica walked off. She sat down with Elizabeth and Amy and Eva. "I really did see a mermaid, you know," she said as she opened the lunch bag Elizabeth passed over to her.

"If you're going to make something up, make up something better," Amy teased. "Why don't you say you saw a man-eating shark?"

"Because I didn't see a man-eating shark, Amy, I saw a mermaid!" Jessica shouted.

A nearby group of boys began laughing. "Did it have a long green scaly tail with flippers?" Charlie Cashman demanded.

"No," Jessica said.

"Was it riding a seahorse?" Ken Matthews teased.

Jessica glared at them. She had never been so angry and embarrassed in her life. Usually she was popular, but today nobody seemed to like her.

"Were there any mer*men* or mer*babies*?" Winston asked. "Cute widdle teensy-weensy merbabies?" The boys laughed.

Tears sprang to Jessica's eyes. "No! But I saw what I saw."

Lila hopped down off her rock and beckoned to Jessica. With a hopeful feeling, Jessica walked over to her friend. She knew Lila was having a bad day too. Maybe Lila was ready to believe her.

"Listen," Lila said in her bossy, grown-up voice. "You better cut it out. Just admit you were making it all up, and everyone will stop teasing you. I'll even let you wear my shell necklace for five minutes."

Jessica gulped hard. More than anything, she wanted everyone to stop teasing her. From the moment school had begun that day, she had felt grumpy and left out.

43

Lila was waiting impatiently. "Well?"

Very slowly Jessica shook her head. She felt terrible. "I'm not making it up," she said in quavering voice. Hanging her head, Jessica turned and walked away from her friends. She saw Ellen wading in the shallow water, still searching for her last shell.

Jessica wished she could help Ellen. But Ellen didn't believe her, so there was no reason to risk getting her fancy new clothes wet with salt water.

With a sigh, Jessica sat down and ate her lunch alone.

CHAPTER 7

Jessica's Promise

Elizabeth polished her apple on her shirt and took a bite. She munched thoughtfully and watched her sister eating lunch by herself. It wasn't like Jessica to keep doing something that made people mad at her. She preferred to have everyone like her.

"I wonder if Jessica is telling the truth," Elizabeth said.

Amy laughed. "Now *you're* going cuckoo."

"No." Elizabeth shook her head. "I don't believe in mermaids. But usually when Jessica plays a joke, she gives up after a while and laughs."

"That's true," Eva agreed. She picked a raisin out of a bag of trail mix. "That's what she did on the bus."

"Now *you* believe it?" Amy asked Eva. "This is too much."

Eva shrugged. "Maybe Jessica really saw *something*."

"But not a mermaid," Amy said quickly.

Elizabeth finished her apple and put the core in her empty lunch bag. "I'm going to figure this out once and for all," she said.

She climbed down off their rock and

crossed the sand to Jessica. "Hi."

"Hi," Jessica replied softly.

"I want to ask you something," Elizabeth began, sitting down beside her sister. "Please tell me the truth. I promise I won't be mad at you. Were you making up that story about the mermaid?"

Jessica's lip trembled. "No," she whispered. "Honest."

"Will you make our special promise sign?" Elizabeth asked to be doubly sure.

"Yes, I will," Jessica said. She crossed her heart and snapped her fingers twice. It was a signal that the twins saved for extra-special and important promises.

"I promise, promise, promise three times that I'm telling the truth," Jessica said.

Elizabeth was puzzled. She scratched her head a moment. "A mermaid?"

"Yes," Jessica said eagerly. "She had brown eyes and long lashes, and long wavy hair, and—"

"Where was it?" Elizabeth asked, more puzzled than ever.

"Way back there." Jessica waved her hand back down the beach. "In a tidal pool."

"Are you sure it wasn't an animal?" Elizabeth asked uncertainly.

"With long wavy hair?" Jessica asked.

"It is mysterious," Elizabeth agreed.

Jessica nodded. "But you do believe me, don't you?"

"I believe you saw something," Eliza-

beth said. "And I'll go with you to talk to Mrs. Otis."

"Yippee!" Jessica threw her arms around Elizabeth. "You're the best sister in the world."

"I sure hope you aren't tricking me again," Elizabeth said.

"No way," Jessica promised, hugging Elizabeth even tighter. "You'll see."

Elizabeth hugged Jessica back. She was pretty confident Jessica wasn't lying, but she still wasn't sure there was a real live mermaid in the tidal pool.

There was only one way to find out.

CHAPTER 8

The Tidal Pool

Together, Jessica and Elizabeth crossed the sand to Mrs. Otis. Their teacher was talking with Travis about whales.

"Hi, girls," Mrs. Otis said when they walked up.

Jessica was glad her sister had confidence in her. It made it easier to face their teacher. "I know I said I saw things that weren't there," Jessica began, "but there really was something in the tidal pool."

Mrs. Otis sighed. "Mermaids are mythic creatures. They exist only in books and movies," the teacher said. She smiled. "It's time to stop joking, Jessica."

"But I'm not joking," Jessica said. "Not anymore."

"I believe her," Elizabeth spoke up.

Mrs. Otis widened her eyes. "Elizabeth, you do?"

Travis was shaking his head and smiling. "Girls, I've been a ranger here for three years. If there were any mermaids, I'd know."

"I don't think it was a mermaid," Elizabeth explained. "But I'm sure Jessica really did see something. Maybe we should find out what it is."

Mrs. Otis looked from Jessica to

Elizabeth and back again. Jessica held her breath.

"I sure hope this isn't a big joke, Jessica," their teacher said. "Or I'll be very disappointed in you."

Jessica nodded anxiously. She knew she had seen something. But what if it wasn't there when they went back?

"I'm not lying, I promise," she whispered.

"OK, we'll go have a look," Mrs. Otis said. She stood up and brushed the sand from her jeans. "Class! Attention, everyone! We're going to walk back a bit to the tidal pool where Jessica thinks she saw a mermaid."

"Oh, no!" some of the kids complained.

"What a waste of time," Winston said.

"Do we have to?" Lila asked. She rolled her eyes at Jessica. "I'm sure the tidal pool is empty."

Jessica's face felt hot. She reached for Elizabeth's hand.

"Come on, let's settle this once and for all," Travis suggested. "Lead the way, girls."

Jessica and Elizabeth walked hand in hand back down the beach. Behind them, Jessica could hear their classmates grumbling.

"What if it isn't there?" Jessica whispered fearfully to Elizabeth. "Everybody will be even madder at me!"

"Don't worry," Elizabeth said, giving Jessica's hand a squeeze. "I won't be mad at you."

Jessica was glad about that. As long as her sister believed her, it didn't matter what anyone else thought. Still, Jessica could feel her stomach starting to get all knotted up.

At last they reached the tidal pool where Jessica had stopped to cool her feet. The pool was very large. When the tide was out, it was like a small ocean of its own, surrounded by rocks.

"It's a deep pool," Travis said as the class spread out around the edge.

"Whoever sees the mermaid first gets five bucks," Charlie teased.

Jessica stared as hard as she could into the water. She could feel her friends looking at her and thinking she was a liar.

"Do you see anything?" Elizabeth whispered to Jessica.

Nervously, Jessica shook her head.

Then Ellen let out a scream. "I found it!"

"Where?" Jessica gasped.

"The mermaid?" Mrs. Otis asked in astonishment.

Ellen knelt down and felt in the water. When she pulled out her hand, she had a smooth yellow cowrie shell in her palm. "I knew I could find one!" she said with a triumphant smile. "I told you, Lila."

"Hmmpph!" Lila muttered, barely looking over.

Jessica could barely look too. She was so disappointed, she wanted to run

away. This was too humiliating.

Then they all heard a faint splash and a snuffling sniff.

"There it is!" Winston yelled.

CHAPTER 9

Mermaid

"I see it, too!" Elizabeth exclaimed. "There by the rock!"

Tangled in some seaweed was a baby sea lion, its brown eyes wide and lonesome. It struggled to the surface to get a gulp of air, and then whisked out of sight behind a rock. Travis stepped down into the water and gently untangled the little animal.

"Is this what you saw, Jessica?" the ranger asked, holding up the sleek brown sea lion pup.

Jessica nodded. Her cheeks were pink with embarrassment. "I guess so," she mumbled.

"You thought it was a mermaid?" Charlie asked with a guffaw. "Gee, I would have said it looked more like a giant sea monster."

Elizabeth put her arm across Jessica's shoulders. "That seaweed looked a lot like hair," she said. "And it has beautiful brown eyes, just like Jessica said. I would have thought the same thing."

"I wouldn't have," Lila announced. "Everyone knows there's no such thing as a mermaid."

"And they sure don't look like sea lions," Ken added, grinning. Many of

the kids were giggling and whispering to each other.

Suddenly Jessica burst into tears. "Quit teasing me!" she sniffed. "I didn't get a close look before!"

"That's all right, Jessica," Mrs. Otis said. She gave Jessica a hug. "You just ignore them. It was an easy mistake to make."

"It's hard to see with the sunshine on the water, right?" Elizabeth added encouragingly.

Jessica sniffled. "It was," she agreed. She sounded a little better.

"I think it's even neater to find a baby sea lion than a mermaid," Eva said.

"I think so too." Amy smiled at Jessica. "It's just the cutest thing I ever saw."

"I wish I'd found it," Elizabeth said,

reaching out to pat the small animal in Travis's arms. Its fur was soft and silky, even though it was soaking wet.

"Why was it trapped? Is it hurt?" Lois asked nervously.

Travis examined the baby sea lion by feeling its legs and tail and checking its eyes. "She seems fine to me," Travis said.

"It's a girl?" Jessica asked, beginning to smile.

"Yes," Travis said. "And she's an orphan. Sometimes these little babies get separated from their moms."

Elizabeth felt a tug of sadness at her heart. "What happened to her mother, Travis?"

"I don't know," the ranger said with a shrug. "She might have been killed by a shark, or trapped in a net, or been sick."

"Poor little baby," Jessica whispered, looking at the orphaned sea lion.

"But she's a lucky little lady," Travis said. He gave Jessica a smile. "If you hadn't seen her, she would have been in real danger when the tide came back in. She would have been swept back out to sea, and she could have been killed too."

"You mean I saved her life?" Jessica asked in astonishment.

"It looks that way," Mrs. Otis said. "She's lucky you were so determined to make us come back here."

Jessica was beaming with pride. "I told you I really saw something," she said confidently.

"What will happen to her now,

Travis?" Elizabeth asked.

The ranger cuddled the baby against his shoulder, and the little animal looked around with curious, big brown eyes. It had the sweetest face Elizabeth had ever seen.

"Fortunately we have a special program for rescuing orphan animals," Travis said. "We take care of them, and try to teach them the same things their moms would in the wild. Then, when they're old enough, we let them loose again so they can live free."

Elizabeth smiled at Jessica. "You're a hero," she said happily.

"You sure are, Jessica," Travis said.

Jessica was smiling from ear to ear.

"One more thing," Travis added. "We

always let the person who finds the orphan give it a name."

"I get to name her?" Jessica asked excitedly.

"I'd call her Lila if I got to name her," Lila said.

Amy made a face. "Good thing you didn't find her."

Lila stuck her tongue out at Amy. Jessica laughed.

"What do you want to call her, Jess?" Elizabeth asked.

Jessica frowned in concentration, while all the kids watched and waited. Then Jessica's eyes sparkled.

"I know," she said. "I'll name her Mermaid."

CHAPTER 10

Happy Feet

"Now I can honestly say I found a mermaid," Jessica explained when everyone just stared at her speechlessly.

Elizabeth let out a laugh. "I can't wait to see the expressions on Mom and Dad's faces when you tell them!"

In a moment, everyone else was laughing too. Travis climbed out of the tidal pool with Mermaid in his arms, and handed her to Jessica.

"Would you like to hold her?" he asked. "She's still wet."

"I don't care!" Jessica cradled the baby animal very carefully. Mermaid looked up at her with wide, innocent eyes. Her whiskers twitched as she sniffed at Jessica's sailor top.

"She's just so sweet!" Ellen said.

"Don't you wish you could keep her?" Eva said.

Soon Jessica was surrounded by all her classmates. Everyone wanted a chance to pet the baby sea lion. Some of the kids even said they had believed there was a mermaid all along.

"I knew you must have seen something," Caroline Pearce, the class know-it-all, said.

"Then why didn't you stick up for her?" Elizabeth asked quickly.

"It doesn't matter anymore," Jessica said. She was just happy to be among her friends again. She snuggled her face in Mermaid's fur and smiled.

"Jessica, why don't you hand Mermaid back to Travis now," Mrs. Otis said after a few minutes. "She probably needs to rest."

Reluctantly Jessica let go of her new friend. Travis began to talk about the habits of sea lions, and Mrs. Otis took Jessica aside. Elizabeth came along.

"We need to have a little talk, Jessica," their teacher said. "Everything worked out well, but it might not have. Have you ever heard of the boy who cried wolf?"

"Yes," Jessica said, hanging her head. She glanced at Elizabeth. Her sister gave her a sympathetic smile.

"Just think," Mrs. Otis continued gently. "Mermaid almost didn't get rescued because no one wanted to believe your story. If only you hadn't played so many jokes before, we would have come right away."

"I know," Jessica said. "I won't do it again."

"Good," Mrs. Otis said, holding out her hand. "Then I promise to believe you the next time you say you've found something important."

Feeling proud and grown-up, Jessica shook the teacher's hand. "It's a deal," she said. "Maybe I'll even rescue another sea lion one day."

"Maybe you will," Mrs. Otis said, smiling. "Now let's go see what the others are talking about."

Jessica felt her smile disappear. Most of the kids were standing in or near the shallow water, looking down while Travis talked about the creatures that lived under the sand.

"I can't," Jessica said sadly. "I'll ruin my shoes."

Caroline walked over and tapped Mrs. Otis's shoulder. "My mom made me bring an extra pair of sneakers," she said. "Jessica can borrow them, if she wants to."

"That's very generous of you, Caroline," Mrs. Otis said.

"Yes, thanks, Caroline. Now Jessica doesn't have to feel so left out anymore," Elizabeth added.

With a happy smile, Jessica sat on a rock to change her shoes. "Now that I can explore, who knows what I'll find!" she said.

Elizabeth giggled. "I think I'll explore with you. If there are any more mermaids, I want to find them too!"

When the twins arrived at school the next day, Ellen was wearing her own shell necklace.

"It's just the same as Lila's," Ellen said with a smile. "And Lila is so mad!"

"You can't even tell them apart," Elizabeth said, admiring Ellen's shells. "Just like me and Jessica."

"That reminds me of something I heard," Ellen said. "Casey's Ice Cream Parlor is having a new kind of sundae called Twin Delight. I saw a sign for it yesterday when my mom and I went to get ice cream."

"Twin Delight?" Jessica repeated. "Liz and I should check it out."

Ellen nodded excitedly. "They're inviting real twins from all around to come and have a free sundae," she explained. "I guess it's kind of an advertising idea."

"Free ice-cream sundaes?" Jessica said, her eyes lighting up eagerly. "Wait till Steven hears about this." Steven was the twins' older brother. His stomach was a bottomless pit. And he loved sundaes—with double everything on them.

Elizabeth smiled. "He's going to be so jealous. But we deserve it. He's always teasing us."

"Maybe if you give him one of your sundaes, he'll stop," Ellen said.

"No way!" Jessica giggled. "Let's forget about him. Just get me to Casey's *fast*!"

Will Steven find a way to get a free sundae? Find out in Sweet Valley Kids #50, **STEVEN'S TWIN.**

SIGN UP FOR THE
SWEET VALLEY HIGH®
FAN CLUB!

Hey, girls! Get all the gossip on Sweet
Valley High's® most popular teenagers
when you join our fantastic Fan Club!
As a member, you'll get all of this really
cool stuff:

- Membership Card with your own
  personal Fan Club ID number
- A Sweet Valley High® Secret
  Treasure Box
- Sweet Valley High® Stationery
- Official Fan Club Pencil (for secret
  note writing!)
- Three Bookmarks
- A "Members Only" Door Hanger
- Two Skeins of J. & P. Coats® Embroidery
  Floss with flower barrette instruction
  leaflet
- Two editions of *The Oracle* newsletter
- Plus exclusive Sweet Valley High®
  product offers, special savings,
  contests, and much more!

Be the first to find out what Jessica & Elizabeth Wakefield are up to by joining the
Sweet Valley High® Fan Club for the one-year membership fee of only $6.25 each
for U.S. residents, $8.25 for Canadian residents (U.S. currency). Includes shipping
& handling.

Send a check or money order (do not send cash) made payable to "Sweet Valley
High® Fan Club" along with this form to:

SWEET VALLEY HIGH® FAN CLUB, BOX 3919-B, SCHAUMBURG, IL 60168-3919

NAME_____
(Please print clearly)

ADDRESS_____

CITY_____ STATE _____ ZIP_____
(Required)

AGE _____ BIRTHDAY_____ /_____ /_____

Offer good while supplies last. Allow 6-8 weeks after check clearance for delivery. Addresses without ZIP
codes cannot be honored. Offer good in USA & Canada only. Void where prohibited by law.
©1993 by Francine Pascal   LCI-1383-123